A Child's DETERMINATION

LIN JESHUA

AuthorHouse™ UK
1663 Liberty Drive
Bloomington, IN 47403 USA
www.authorhouse.co.uk
Phone: 0800 047 8203 (Domestic TFN)
+44 1908 723714 (International)

Because of the dynamic nature of the Internet, any web addresses or links contained in this book may have changed since publication and may no longer be valid. The views expressed in this work are solely those of the author and do not necessarily reflect the views of the publisher, and the publisher hereby disclaims any responsibility for them.

This book is printed on acid-free paper.

ISBN: 978-1-5049-8746-2 (sc)
ISBN: 978-1-7283-8519-8 (e)

Print information available on the last page.

Published by AuthorHouse 09/20/2019

authorHOUSE®

I dedicate this book to my Children who are always great and have inspired me to write this book. I could never ask for better children than these. God bless their precious souls

I may not always express it enough but My heartfelt thanks to my Husband who is kind, generous and always supportive.

Many thanks and appreciation to Libby Charlton for her for valuable advice, time taken in helping out with editing this book during the editing period, much appreciated.

Frank Nyoni, thank you so very much for putting in a few hours of your time proofreading my script. Much appreciated.

Finally, I would like to appreciate and express my gratitude to Author house for all the work they put into the creation of this book, the support, advice and encouragement they gave is such wonderful. It has been a pleasure working with them.

I Am Driven to reach my goals and exceed my own limitations as I learn from those who love and care to see me growing and developing into an amazing person of tomorrow

DEAN

The early hours of Saturday morning were bright and sunny as I lay in my bed with eyes wide open, trying hard to contain the excitement which was threatening to gush out of my little lungs. At the same time, I willed everyone else in the house to wake up.

"How can they still be snoring?" I said quietly to myself. "Don't they remember what day it is? Surely, they should remember."

By now, I began to fidget restlessly, turning and tossing under my bedcovers. You would think I was dancing to the soft musical sounds made by the graceful birds, which could clearly be heard through the brick walls of our old maisonette flat, all the way from the neighbouring farms and the beautiful Farmoor Reservoir.

On listening closely, the harmonious sounds all sounded so lovely. At first, I could not recognise the tune, but, suddenly, as though a water tap had been turned on, I found myself singing along as the tune became clearer and more distinct.

I wondered if people knew that birds were the most talented musicians ever. The realisation took me by surprise.

The song continued: "Happy birthday to you, happy birthday to you".

The broad smile that formed on my lips kept widening; I could burst with joy.

"What a beautiful day!" I said, jumping off the bed as if I had been electrocuted.

There was no way I could stay there a minute longer. I just could not. What child would? Well, one thing was for sure: it wasn't going to be me. I raced to the living room.

In my imagination, I was already munching on that yummy, gooey chocolate cake, savouring every mouthful before chewing and swallowing it.

Mm! What a yummy, yummy cake! Oh, it tastes so good. It's like nothing from this world and is definitely from another planet.

I wonder if aliens made it on their secret alien planet, I thought. *Maybe I should go live with aliens; then, I can eat as much chocolate cake as I want, whenever I want.*

Who could blame me? It wasn't my fault that I was born with such a sweet tooth. I loved everything sweet. What child doesn't? Sometimes Mum would yell at me for not eating my savoury meals, preferring instead to dive straight into the dessert. That made Mum and Dad decide not to buy any sweet desserts.

Now, at the age of seven, my teeth were beginning to give me a taste of my own medicine. Oh, I hated those visits to the dentist that Mum forced upon us every six months.

"Aargh!" I exclaimed aloud. "When is everyone going to wake up? I am super tired of waiting."

I moped as I roughly threw myself into the armchair, sitting there without taking notice of Mum's warnings.

"Dee, stop jumping on the furniture like that!" she usually said. "Can't you see that you're damaging it? If I ever catch anyone doing that again, you will go on the discipline stool in the dark corner over there."

We never took any notice of Mum unless her tone of voice rose to a serious one. Then, like naughty dogs with our tails between our legs, we would do as she said.

By now, up from the chair, I had finished my fantasy of munching down the cake and moved on to the next exciting thing: opening the presents. I imagined opening them one by one, throwing the wrappers everywhere.

This was so much fun! Better than tossing and turning on the bed. I had no idea what time it was; it just didn't matter to me. All I cared about was seeing everyone up and about.

After what seemed like a million years, the melodious harmonies of the birds could hardly be heard anymore. They were replaced by sounds of passing cars on the road outside. Inside the house, doors opened. My parents emerged from their room, and the living room was soon filled with happy faces.

"Morning, Mum; morning, Dad," I hurriedly said, not even taking a breath or waiting for a response.

Whether or not they responded was irrelevant. I was on a mission. And very eager.

"Mum! Mum! Is Girlie-Girlie still sleeping?" I asked enthusiastically.

"Yes, Dee, and don't you dare wake her up! She will wake up in her own good time," Mum replied.

She knew what I was like and decided to give me a warning before I could run into the bedroom I shared with my baby sister and carry her into the living room.

Why didn't I wake her up earlier, when I got up? It would have been easier than having to wait for her now, I thought.

"Aaaargh! But, Mum." Mum paid no attention, so I turned towards Dad. "Dad, shall I go bring Girlie-Girlie to eat her breakfast?"

I knew Dad wouldn't mind; he had always been the softer one of the two. Dad would always understand and give in to our pleas, especially if we made a pleading face.

I hurriedly ate my breakfast. That day, Mum didn't even sing her usual go-brush-your-teeth song. As soon as I'd finished eating, I ran to the bathroom and quickly brushed my teeth. I had never brushed my teeth at that speed. I even surprised myself!

As I was finishing, suddenly I heard, "Happy birthday, Girlie-Girlie!"

I quickly threw the toothbrush into the basin and rushed to the living room. I went straight to my baby sister, gave her a huge hug, and wished her a wonderful birthday.

"Dee, leave her alone, and be careful not to drop her!" Mum said as I lifted my sister off the floor and swung her up in the air.

Bless Susanna—my little sister's real name—she looked so confused, not understanding what the fuss was all about.

She smiled and answered in her sweet, lovely voice, "'Appy birthday."

She was now three years old and still could not pronounce some of her words properly. She seemed to enjoy the attention she was getting and the commotion going on around the house.

"Mummy! Mummy, it's almost evening now. When is the party going to start?"

It was barely midday, but it seemed like the day was already coming to an end. Clearly, I was rushing the hours away.

Mum would not bother entertaining my excitement. Instead, she said, "Dee, would you please settle down and calm yourself a bit? If you continue like this, you will go read a book."

What?! Was she serious? No chance that I would read a book on a day like this. She must be joking.

I knew better than to push my luck. Turning to the TV, I picked up the remote control and turned on my favourite programme and watched, at the same time wishing and praying for the birthday celebrations to start.

Mum went through her house chores at what seemed like tortoise speed. Then, lunch was served, and we all dived in. I didn't bother to wash my hands; when Mum asked, I just mumbled that I had. No one would know whether I had washed them or not, so no one could argue that I hadn't.

Mum cleared the table. Most of the time, she would ask us to take our plates to the sink. This would test her patience, as it would take all her energy to get us to help with chores around the house.

As she was loading the dishwasher, a soft ringing melody rang from her mobile phone. I loved the ringtone on Mum's phone. She had one of those calm lullabies and would always turn it on when she put Girlie-Girlie to bed, leaving it playing quietly whilst she fell asleep.

Mum hardly ever sang out loud. Once, she told us that when she was growing up, she had loved singing. Whenever she sang, her dad, my grandpa, would come running to check who was crying, and why, only to find Mum singing joyfully and without a care in the world.

I quickly picked up the phone and ran towards Mum, calling out to her, "Mum, Mum, your phone! Your phone is ringing."

She gently took it and said, "Thank you, Pumpkin."

Mum always called Susanna and me Pumpkin whenever we did something that she appreciated; otherwise, she would just use our names or Susanna's pet name of Girlie-Girlie.

I had always been called Dee at home, short for Dean. As I got older, I was no longer so keen on the nickname, especially on school pick-ups when Mum would call out, "Dee, come on, let's go!" This caused all my friends and their parents to look over with inquiring eyes to see who was being called. I was beginning to feel a bit grown up, being called in public that way, instead I preferred it to be with my full name.

Mum said into the phone, "Hello."

After that, there was silence as she listened.

A little while later, I heard her say, "Oh! Sure, you can come. It's fine."

Although Mum had cleaned the house that morning, the place was now a mess, with toys, shoes, and other bits and pieces scattered all over. As we went in and out, we would wear one pair of shoes and later on get another pair. If one of the shoes got kicked under the table or sofa, we wouldn't bother picking them up; instead, we would just get another pair. My baby sister and I would play games and not bother picking up after ourselves when we had finished playing. We left it all for Mum to clear up.

I thought that we were too young to do chores. At the age of seven, surely, I was still very young, let alone my baby sister who had just turned three that morning.

Mum called out, "Dee, Girlie-Girlie, please pick up all your toys, games, and the shoes which you left lying around—now! I want that room spotless. Aunt Jenny is coming."

Mum didn't like relatives or friends coming around our house and find it in a state.

"This place looks like a World War II bomb has landed and blasted it," she would usually say.

"Ah! But, Mum, we're watching—"

Mum continued scolding us, but Susanna and I were curled up comfortably on the sofas, obviously not bothered by Mum's urgent instructions. We were watching our favourite programme, and nothing would make us move, not even an inch.

"Oh no, you don't!" retorted Mum, clearly annoyed that I had not moved to tidy up.

I could hardly keep myself from bursting into giggles. If only Mum could see her face; she looked so funny every time she tried to make a serious facial expression. She looked as though she had guzzled down a cupful of iced water!

"Tidy up now, or—"

"Or no TV all week," Girlie-Girlie said, mimicking Mum.

Dad burst out laughing on hearing Girlie-Girlie finish off Mum's sentence. All along, he had been busy working on the computer in front of him. Goodness knows what he was doing on that computer all day.

Does he always take notice of everything that happens around? I wondered

"Tidy up now, or you will never do blah, blah, blah" had turned into Mum's daily anthem.

Over time, we had learnt that when Mum started with the threats, she meant them. We reluctantly began picking up our mess, one thing at a time. Have you ever seen slow-motion movement? That was how fast our feet moved. A tortoise would have been faster than we were. We had perfected that tactic so well over time! We had come to realise that, as the minutes ticked by, Mum would then swiftly tidy up, so that by the time a visitor arrived, the house would be in perfect order. We never put much effort in at all. Why would we?

As we returned to watching TV, there was a loud knock on the door. We leapt up and sped towards the door, screaming, "Aunt Jenny! Aunt Jenny!"

We loved it so much when Aunt Jenny visited; she was always kind to us. Before her dog, Rosie, died, she used to take us along to walk her around our village reservoir. Sometimes she would drive us in her car to the neighbouring village where she lived, and we would play till we were exhausted. She always gave us chocolates and sweets when we went to her house.

We're having the time of our lives! we thought whilst swinging on the swings, bouncing on see-saws, horse riding, and monkey climbing—you name it. I am pretty sure that, when it came to playing, we were the best, just the two of us.

The door opened, and Aunt Jenny came in. Behold! What on earth was she carrying? I had never seen such a massive present.

What could it be? I wondered, perplexed.

As soon as her eyes rested on my baby sister, Aunt Jenny said breathlessly, "Happy birthday, Susanna!"

Aunt Jenny struggled to get the enormous package through the door and into the living room. The parcel was as big and tall as she was!

I wasn't keen to hear the happy birthday song or wishes; I was sure we'd had enough of that already.

"What is it? What is it?!" I screamed with excitement, at the same time stretching my hands out to grab the present. It was apparent how excited I was.

"Just hold your horses, Dee," Mum said as she came through to greet Aunt Jenny. "You know it's not yours; let Susanna take it. It was her birthday last time I checked."

How could Mum say that? I wondered to myself. *Didn't I open Girlie-Girlie's presents for her the last two years?*

"Thank you," Susanna said to Aunt Jenny.

Susanna always remembered to say "thank you" when given something, unlike me. I needed constant reminders to remember such words even existed.

It had always seemed like a losing battle for Mum. Frequently, she would ask, "Dee, what do you say?"

Aunt Jenny explained the gift to Mum after she had uncovered it. "Lynne, I saw this tiger at a charity shop, and I thought that Susanna would love it, since she has a thing for soft toys and Tigers."

"I love it, I love it, and I love it!" screamed Susanna, jumping up and down before Mum could even say a word.

"Well, Susanna, you know very well that when adults are talking, you don't interrupt, don't you?" Mum said, clearly not happy with Susanna's behaviour.

"Aunt Jenny, I'm sure she will love to have it, as you can see. Thank you so much for getting it for her," Mum said.

After that, Aunt Jenny and Mum talked for a few more minutes.

Aunt Jenny then left, explaining that she was, in fact, in a bit of a hurry and couldn't stay for a cuppa.

Girlie-Girlie and I were now busy playing with the tiger toy, climbing on her back and riding on her. We had so much fun, as we had something new and totally different from our usual toys. The tiger was enormous. I loved the dark vertical stripes that ran down the reddish-orange soft fur, which was enjoyable to rub.

"Girlie-Girlie, what are you going to name your tiger?" Mum asked.

Why do toys have to have names, anyway? Who on earth came up with that idea? Some things were just too weird for my brain to understand; we just wanted to play, not start thinking about naming the toy!

"Double. Her name is Double," Susanna said, continuing to bounce up and down on the tiger's back.

"Hmm, interesting. Why Double, then?" Mum asked, curious to learn Susanna's reasons behind the name she had chosen.

"Oh! Because she is gigantic, Mummy. Can't you see?" I said, without giving it a second thought as I thought that must have been Susanna's logic reasoning behind the name. She had found it so funny a few months back when we had laughed our lungs out as dad told a story of how his friend's cousin from Africa had named his son 'CornerKick' as his first name only because his favourite football player was so talented on scoring goals during match games from a corner kick. Apparently in some cultures names can be given to children or animals, especially dogs according to events happening at the time the child is born or the Dog is acquired.

Mum disliked it whenever I spoke on Susanna's behalf. This had been a habit of mine since Susanna was born. Mum would often ask if I was her mouthpiece. She was my baby sister, and I always felt that I knew what she would say if she were able to talk. At first, Mum didn't seem to mind my assumed responsibility, but as the months turned into years, Susanna didn't bother to talk, as she knew that I would speak for her. It then became a bit of a concern when she turned two and still could not talk much, except for a very few words. At this point, she was booked in for speech and language therapy. After the first session, she started going to nursery, and her communication started to improve bit by bit as she gained confidence in herself.

"Dee, I'm not asking you. Are you Susanna? Let her speak for herself for once; you're not her mouthpiece. I keep telling you that."

People who knew me always thought that I could be the Guinness World Record holder in my age group for talking nonstop. Aunt Nicki called me a chatterbox, as my mouth was constantly itching to say something.

"Dee, I am talking to you, and I expect a response. Do you hear me?"

"I hear you crystal clear, Mother, but Girlie-Girlie doesn't mind me speaking for her. Do you mind, Girlie-Girlie?" I said, unbothered by Mum's scolding.

Meanwhile, Susanna wasn't showing any interest in the conversation that was going on between me and Mum; instead, she kept on bouncing on that tiger. She was in her own world.

At times, I could tell that Mum got emotionally tired from our energetic activities.

"Double's her name, then! Now take her to your room because she can't stay in here," Mum instructed, visibly tired from the energy we were displaying.

"Why, but why?" Susanna asked, her eyes glistening with tears which threatened to fall at any second.

Although Susanna would not speak much, her favourite, perfected phrase was to ask why. No matter how you answered her, she would continue to ask "why" until you were tired of trying to explain things to her. I doubt if Girlie-Girlie even understood the meaning and proper use of the word.

"Susanna," Mum said, kneeling down in front of her, "There isn't much space in here. It will be much better if Double stays in your room."

As I stood there, still looking at Double, I thought my mind was playing tricks on me. Was there a teardrop in Double's eye? Did my eyes deceive me? It couldn't be! The tiger was only a toy! Wasn't she made of fabric? It was crazy to think a toy could show any emotions, let alone shed a tear. No way could she cry. Only people can cry. It was impossible.

Unaware of the drama unfolding before my eyes, Susanna grabbed Double, stormed out of the living room, and ran to our bedroom, upset that she was not allowed to play with Double in the living room. Susanna hated playing far away from everybody.

"Mum, she can't get through! Double can't get through the door to our room. She's too big!" Susanna called out in a quivering voice, on the verge of tears.

"Really? OK, I will help you," Mum said, heading towards our bedroom.

I followed close behind Mum.

Picking up Double in her arms, Mum squeezed her through the doorway and into our bedroom. Once inside, she placed Double in the corner, next to Susanna's bed, telling her she would have to put the tiger there once she'd finished playing with her.

The tears were soon forgotten as I went to play with Susanna whilst patiently waiting for the party. We took turns climbing on Double and riding on her back.

We screamed, "Horsy! Horsy!" as we jumped up and down on the bed, where we had placed Double for an even more bouncy effect.

It was such good fun playing with Double, and I loved it.

In the early evening, Aunt Nicki came over with her two-year-old daughter, Ruth. Not far behind them, Aunt Rosa and Aunt Helen also arrived, and it was time for the long-awaited party and birthday celebration.

Mum had cooked a scrumptious dinner, which had taken her hours to prepare, but it was well worth it.

The living room was beautifully decorated with party decorations in a Doc McStuffins theme. A personalised banner across the wall read, "Happy Third Birthday, Most Beautiful Susanna"; matching balloons hung on either side of the banner. There were Doc McStuffins pieces decorating the dinner table too. The theme had been chosen because Susanna would spend hours glued to the TV, watching Doc McStuffins, an animated series that she loved.

As we sat down to eat, my focus was beyond the food in front of me—I could only think about the cake. I hurriedly ate my food, encouraging everyone to eat fast so that the cake could be served.

Aunt Nicki had to ask me to stop rushing them, saying that they would take their time eating, as the cake would not grow legs and run away. When she said that, everyone fell about laughing, which didn't sit well with me. I just wanted the cake!

I thought about screaming, "Cake, cake, where are you?"

I just could not wait for everyone to finish their meal; there was so much food! Barbecue chicken wings and glazed barbecue pork ribs; side dishes of roast potatoes, carrots, parsnips, sweet potato, coleslaw, egg & potato salad, beetroot salad; fish fingers, chips and slices of pizza. It was a feast where Mum had made our favourite dishes, and we could choose to eat whatever we liked.

I would love to come face to face with the person who said that after eating their main meal, people needed to relax a little before dessert was served; that evening, my patience was really tested. As soon as dinner was cleared, Aunt Nicki suggested that a dance song be played, and we all took to the dance floor to let our dinner settle before dessert. Either this was a normal routine to let a meal settle first, or my family used it as a way to discourage my love for sweet desserts—I just wondered.

The soft music playing in the background was replaced with more-energetic music, which brought everyone to their feet in a dance routine. I could have laughed watching Mum and the other adults carrying on like children at that moment. All except Aunt Helen, who refused to dance, arguing that she wasn't much of a dancer (although she had never lifted her feet to try—ever!). She just sat there, laughing and watching others. Dad tried, but it became evident that he wasn't much of a dancer, as he kept bumping into everyone and stepping on their toes. At one point, he missed his footing, stumbled about, and finally landed on the floor, which made everyone laugh.

After what seemed like a lifetime, the song came to an end, and everyone found a seat. Out of breath from all the dancing, I casually turned to Aunt Nicki and asked if it was time for Girlie-Girlie to cut her cake. Mum gave in and asked Aunt Nicki to do the honours and bring out the cake. I'm sure they had agreed on this beforehand, as Mum just gave Aunt Nicki a nod, and she, in turn, stood up and went into the kitchen. A few minutes later, Aunt Nicki came back, holding that scrumptious cake, glowing with lit candles.

As Aunt Nicki entered the living room, everyone joined in the song which she started:

Happy Birthday to you,
Happy Birthday to you,
Happy Birthday dear Susanna,
Happy Birthday to you.

How old are you now?
How old are you now?
How old are you now Susanna?
How old are you now?

There was a pause as all eyes fell on Girlie-Girlie, with the expectation for her to sing her answer in return.

After two seconds of waiting, the others got what they expected: of course, my voice declaring, at the highest pitch, "I am three years old now!"

I didn't really sing it, so much as scream it out at the top of my voice.

Mum turned and looked at me. "Dee!"

She didn't even finish what she'd wanted to say, as Aunt Nicki resumed the song:

> We wish you many more,
> We're so glad God made you,
> We're so glad God made you,
> Happy Birthday to you.

After the hip-hip hoorays, Susanna was encouraged to blow out the candles and to make a wish.

I kept on thinking, *Why the hassle? Just blow out the candles! Cut the cake, and give it to me—I'll show you what to do with it!*

Susanna's cake was topped with a Doc McStuffins iced doll. The cake did not disappoint my eager taste buds; it definitely lived up to my earlier imaginations. I probably would have eaten the whole lot, but Mum would not allow me to have a second piece. I'd already had the largest piece, and, according to Mum, it was more than enough to last me whole week.

I did not take any notice of what she said; instead, I announced that it was time to open presents for Susanna. I assumed this responsibility, as usual.

"Come on, Dee, let Susanna open her own presents! It's her birthday after all," everyone said all at once, disapproving of what I was about to do.

I had always opened presents for Girlie-Girlie, from her first birthday! I did not understand all the fuss. Why couldn't everyone leave things the way they had always been?

Susanna picked up her presents one by one and started ripping the gift wrappers.

Before long, my help was required to cut fasteners and to put batteries in some of the toys. I was once again in charge. Soon, we were in full force, exploring and playing with all the toys she had received.

As the evening drew to a close, I thought to myself that it had been the best evening. Mum didn't even ask us to help with clearing up after dinner, as Aunt Nicki had volunteered herself for the task. As everyone was leaving, we thanked them and bid them goodbye, then continued playing with Double. Our cousin Ruth had the best time bouncing and tumbling on her.

It was well into the night when we finally changed into our pyjamas and got ready for bed. The excitement was still bubbling over. One thing I knew was that there would never be any more turning and tossing if I woke up a bit early: Double was now there to ride on. No more Mr Boredom—ever.

My wild subconscious transported me into a beautiful dream where Susanna, Ruth, the tiger, and I were playing tug of war. The rope was very strong, made of three strands and cross stitched. Ruth and I were team Y, and Susanna and Double were team Z. Team Z seemed stronger than team Y. No matter how hard we tried to pull them across the line, we just could not overpower them. We lost, and they won, over and over.

It became apparent that the tiger was much stronger than we had anticipated. To test our suspicions, we decided that all three of us would play against Double.

Lo and behold, it turned out that we were right. Double was very strong and would not be moved, not even an inch. We pulled and pulled, but Double still did not budge. She just stood there, holding the rope steady. After a while, she gave a big tug, and we all went tumbling down to the ground. The noise of us falling could be heard from far away.

"Ha! Ha! Ha! Ha! Look at them being beaten by a toy. Ha! Ha! Ha!"

It felt like the ground was laughing at us. Double had won. I could not belie-e-e-eve what had just happened! How was it possible? Surely, three of us must be stronger than one big soft toy.

"Aargh! Poor you, did you think for a minute that you were stronger than me? Not a chance," boasted Double, clearly feeling a deep sense of satisfaction in herself.

"Shall I help you up?" she said, extending her paw towards me.

There was nothing I longed for more than to wipe the grin she was wearing off her face.

We quickly pulled ourselves up and dusted off our clothes, running off towards Mum's voice calling us.

"Dee, Susanna, wake up! Go bathe, and make sure you don't leave your clothes lying around. Make your beds before leaving your room."

I jumped as Mum's voice pierced my ears, waking me up from the dream. It was already morning. Boy, how relived was I to realise that I had been dreaming and none of the events were real.

We let Mum know we were up and we started to get ourselves ready. It was Sunday morning, and we were going to go to church. This was exciting, but we still needed to complete our loathed chores before we left.

More often than not, I would use every excuse in the book to avoid carrying out chores. Occasionally, my excuses worked, especially if they were about doing some kind of school homework. Mum did not often fall for my deceitful excuses, though; she would be firm in her orders. Thus, I would half-heartedly do whatever chore needed to be done, keeping myself as lifeless as I could be. I was happier when left alone to watch my favourite TV programme or to play with my toys till dusk.

Contrary to my usual slapdash approach to chores, Mum chose to do things differently. She emphasised doing things properly, be it folding and packing away clothes, brushing teeth, washing up plates, and even cleaning the cooker. Mum expected things to be left in good order and in perfect condition.

"It's not the end result that matters the most," she would say, "but how you achieve those end results."

Once, after I had finished combing my hair, Mum asked, "Is that the best you can do with your hair, Dee? Did you look at yourself in the mirror? See? The comb missed here and there. You've got to be proud of yourself; you have to look at yourself and feel good about who you are as a person. Don't just do things for the sake of doing them or throw anything on yourself and be content. You have to try to teach yourself to look good and aim for the best. Don't just settle for average; set yourself for only the very best. When you do your school homework, do it well and with your heart in it. When you talk to others, think first about what you are saying. Find pleasure, satisfaction, and enjoyment in what you do."

You would think she would get tired of preaching, but she would carry on and on.

"There is time for everything. TV, Wii, and video games won't put food on your table. There is more to life than just playing and having fun every second of every minute."

Mum was so convinced that children needed to be trained in life skills at a very tender age. She believed that if children grew up without knowing how to care for and look after themselves, it would let them down and be a sign of adverse parental guidance. So, although she was a little bit tough on us, I somehow knew that she wanted the best for us—and out of us—so that we would be better adults of tomorrow. I secretly adored her for that.

We had finished dressing up for church and were all seated around the table, eating breakfast. Usually, Mum had to remind us day after day to sit down whilst eating, but we always roamed around, taking no notice of the scolding. At times, she would have us sit on the discipline corner by ourselves, away from everyone else, for ten minutes or until we apologised.

Susanna and I hated the disciplinary corner wholeheartedly. Even though it was a means for us to correct our ways, we felt that it robbed ten minutes of our playtime. Soon, we learnt to read the signs that would lead to us being put in the disciplinary corner, and then, on detecting the sign, we would immediately calm down.

"Mum, can Double come and sit with us while we eat?" Susanna asked.

"Of course not, Girlie-Girlie. As I already have said, Double is to stay in your room," Mum answered.

The atmosphere turned sour within a second. I loved having Double around, and so did Susanna. We could not protest our unhappiness, so, with long, sad faces we began eating our breakfast. Dad hadn't joined us as yet but before long we could hear his footsteps approaching

"Woo! How should I attempt to get into the living room with this tiger blocking the door?" exclaimed Dad, trying to jump over the big tiger who was comfortably blocking the doorway.

Puzzled by dad's sudden and unexpected remark, Susanna. and I quickly diverted our attention from eating to dad as mum turned towards his direction, at the door. Without a mistake: Double was right there.

Susanna rapidly stood up and rushed over to Double.

"Oh! Double is here!" I said, surprised to see Double sitting by the living room entrance.

Susanna was so ecstatic to see Double, she forgot that Double wasn't supposed to be there and that we were going to be in trouble with Mum.

"Who brought Double in here?" Mum asked in an unpleasant voice, remembering that she had told us that Double was to stay in our room.

"Not me," I quickly said, knowing what was to come as a result for breaking Mum's rule.

Mum took it as a sign of disrespect when we did the opposite of what she said. She never liked repeating herself; actions had to follow her instructions all the time. But, as children, at times, we just didn't do as we were expected to; we loved to mess around and wind our parents up. It was a fun game, but not this time.

"Not me, Mummy. I left Tiger in my bed," Susanna said, calling Double "Tiger" because she was scared of getting into trouble. and reverted into using 'Tiger' an attempt to convince mum how truthful and honest she was rather than using 'Double' a given pet name which she thought would imply that she was still in a playful mode

Mum looked straight in our eyes for some time, then told us to sit quietly and eat our food. It always baffled me how Mum could tell simply by looking at us whether we were telling the truth or lying to her. In most cases, she got it right.

Susanna reluctantly returned to the table, bringing Double with her. Susanna hesitated at her seat, clearly afraid of what Mum would say. Fortunately, Mum didn't say anything. Susanna then placed Double on the floor next to her, putting some of her breakfast in a small plate and placing it in front of Double.

Once settled, we all concentrated on eating our breakfast. Mum, as usual, was having a conversation with Dad about the plans for the day; she loved to plan everything so precisely.

"I'll see what I can do about that," Dad said, giving Mum a vague answer to whatever she had asked him to do. Dad loved to do things in his own time. It didn't matter to him whether something was done immediately or a week or a month later, as long as it was done. We probably got Dad's laid-back genes.

As soon as we finished eating, Susanna and I left the table, rushing off to our room and pulling Double along, not bothering to clear off our plates from the table, even though we were always required to do so after every meal.

"You did not thank Mum for cooking for you, or Dad for providing the food."

The voice did not sound like Susanna's; it was a strange voice I had not heard before and did not recognise.

Susanna seemed terrified; she quickly ran over and hid behind me.

I thought for a minute. Was I imagining things or we were being invaded by an unseen alien?

Who on earth had spoken? as far as I could tell, the voice was nothing like a human voice. We were both baffled by this mystery sound and started to search our room. When it became apparent that neither of us had spoken, I was convinced we were being invaded, but why and by whom? The more I thought about it, the more scared I got, and I started to tremble.

"Boo! I got you!" Double screamed from behind us.

Kneeling to check under the bed, we couldn't see her, so this caused us to turn round in panic.

There was Double, making a funny face at us.

"You gave me a scare," I said, punching Double on the shoulder lightly.

"Me too," declared Susanna.

Mum called us into the living room, announcing that she was going to get dressed and wanted both of us to tidy up the dining table. She had picked up her plate and Dad's and taken them to the kitchen, leaving mine and Susanna's, to drive the point home that she would never back down on her instructions.

"Yes, Mum, we will definitely do that!" I said.

"That will be the first time ever, if these two do as they are told today, knowing what they are like," Dad said, clearly doubting us.

Once they were gone, we went back to our room and turned towards Double, only to find that she was glaring at us.

"Double, you can speak!" Susanna said with excitement as soon as puzzlement wore off.

"Can you walk? Did you walk to the living room earlier on? Wow! This is cool! I never had a toy that could walk and talk in real life."

"What did you expect? That I would be your horsy-horsy kind of toy?" said Double, implying that she wasn't keen on being jumped on, up and down, all day long.

"Mum! Dad! Mum!" called Susanna.

"What are you calling Mum and Dad for?" I said, closing Girlie-Girlie's mouth with my hands to stop her from attracting unnecessary attention from our parents.

"Listen, let's keep this to ourselves for now, till we know more about the strange talking tiger here," I told my sister.

"I can hear you. Remember, I am just right in front of you," Double said.

I didn't take notice of the tiger speaking at that moment. I wanted to make sure Girlie-Girlie was on board with my suggestion. Moreover, I wanted to discover the secret and intentions behind this toy's talking ability.

Susanna looked at me for a good while without answering.

I finally grasped her shoulder and asked, "Girlie-Girlie, do you hear me?"

"All right, I won't tell."

"Susanna, promise," I said at the same time that Girlie-Girlie forcefully pushed my hand away.

"I promise, I promise," Susanna said, making a pinkie promise.

"OK, we will keep this our own secret, Girlie-Girlie. Our very own secret. I know you love having a secret."

Dad entered our room just as I had finished speaking.

Susanna and I quickly composed ourselves.

"What are you two whispering about? And where is my shoe brush, Dee?" asked Dad.

"I never touched it," I said

"You never touched it? Did I ask if you touched it? The brush didn't just jump out the window and fly away!"

Dad knew I had the habit of using his shoe brush to brush off my hair, which I usually wore cut short.

After looking around, the brush was found stashed in my school bag, which meant I had hurriedly taken it and brushed my hair on my way to school.

Dad grabbed it, telling me, "Never take this again, Dee, if you can't be bothered to return it."

"Hurry up! We need to get going, kids. We can't be late," Mum announced.

Double turned to us.

"Forgot something?"

"What?" Susanna asked.

"The dining table, remember? Now go, both of you. Mum has told you hundreds of times about cleaning up after yourselves."

Susanna didn't protest, but I wasn't happy at all.

"If you don't go, I will scream!"

"Scream, for all I care," I said.

As soon as I said that, Double let out a blisteringly loud, thunderous yell, which left me shaking.

Mum and Dad ran outside to investigate where the noise was coming from, but, surprisingly, everything seemed peaceful.

"Now go tidy up the table," Double warned.

Reluctantly, I went and helped Susanna, who had already taken the plates. I got the cleaning cloth and started to wipe down the table.

When Mum and Dad found me cleaning, they looked at me with surprised expressions on their faces. They then glanced at each other but, apparently, decided not to make any comment.

We finished cleaning up and went back to our room where we had left Double. As soon as I got there, I went straight to Double with a serious look on my face. I told her that she should not think that she was in charge; no one had appointed her to be a sister-in-charge over us—ever.

Double did not take notice or even acknowledge what I had said to her. I turned to leave, not bothered by her nonresponse. I had said what I needed to say, and that was it. I was intrigued by her demeanour, though. She seemed calm, kind even, yet scary at the same time.

I was somehow eager to find out who she really was. I mean, was she some kind of super magic alien from whatever alien planet? What did she want with us? What I dreaded was having another version of Mum emphasising cleanliness and endless life skills. Though I adored Mum for trying to prepare us for life ahead, I was still bothered by having to do chores and constantly hearing about what I should do in life. The idea of preparing for tomorrow wasn't appealing to me at this age. Going to school was enough for now. I wanted to just enjoy being a child. The future would see for itself at the due time, when I got to that stage.

"Dee, you can't prepare and be ready for the future in the future; you have to do it now." Mum would always try to drive that message into my brain.

We finally left the house and went to church. After the service, we came home. Susanna and I asked if we could go play at the playpark; my baby sister was keen on taking Double along so that she could play with the tiger in a bigger space. Mum usually went with us and would sit at a distance on the benches, reading a book or catching up on emails on her mobile.

There were lots of young children who had come out to play that afternoon. A certain boy decided to go on the monkey bars. Whilst he was swinging from one, slipped off as he tried to catch on the next bar, it just so happened that for some unknown reason Girlie-Girie had left Double there. As the Boy landed, Double swiftly rolled over, so the boy landed on her and was left uninjured.

It seemed no one else noticed Double rolling herself. The mother of the boy thanked Girlie-Girlie for having placed her toy at that place, which had saved her son from a possible bad accident.

Well played, Double, I thought, grinning to myself, puzzled by how she'd managed to move without anyone else noticing. She was indeed a mystery.

One after the other, the days went by. Every time Double would challenge us to do our chores as asked, I typically just ignored her, choosing to carry on playing. She would threaten to draw some attention from Mum and Dad, leaving me extremely unhappy with her being around. Once our chores were completed, Double would let us climb on her and bounce as much as we liked, even though she made sure we were aware she was not just a "horsy toy", as she put it. She also made sure she gave us as much help with our homework as possible. Double believed in education, just like Mum.

It was rare to find Mum sleeping before the end of the day. If that happened, it meant she was very ill. This was the case one particular day when Mum came from work not looking well. Apart from getting us to do chores and homework, Mum always loved to laugh and tell jokes. Unlike Dad, who was a bit quiet and reserved.

"Mum, you don't look so well. Shall I call Dad at work and tell him to come home?" I asked.

I loved my mum. Actually, I loved every member of my family, and I never wanted to see any of them unwell or unhappy.

"No, don't call him. All I need is a good rest, and I will be as good as new when I get up," Mum assured me and Girlie-Girlie, who kept on following Mum, holding onto the hem of the jacket Mum was still wearing.

Mum was literally dragging her feet to get by around the house, and it was noticeable how much effort she was putting into every step she took. Once she got herself into her bedroom, she gave instructions on the food we were to have: fish fingers and chips, which I knew how to cook in the oven.

As soon as Mum closed her bedroom door behind her, I turned on the Wii game and got myself lost in the game. Cooking was long forgotten. I could never go hungry when playing; surprisingly, though, as soon as I finished, hunger would always strike.

By the time I got tired of playing, it was dark outside. Remembering Mum's instructions, I went to the kitchen, which I was surprised to see was spotlessly clean. It was a few minutes before our bedtime.

Looking in the freezer, I saw no fish fingers or chips.

"Girlie-Girlie, where is our food?" I asked, looking in the oven.

Instead of getting a reply from Susanna, I got a tap on the shoulder from behind. I wasn't surprised to see Double looking at me when I spun around, but I was surprised to find out what had happened to the food.

In a gentle whisper, Double asked, "When did you cook the food you're asking about and looking for?"

"I ... I ... " I managed hesitantly. "Double, why are you even asking me that? I saw Susanna taking some food to Mum and bringing back the plates later. I need to eat and then go to sleep."

"Go ask Mum where your food is, then," replied Double.

"Unbelievable!" I said. "You can't cook and eat everything without dishing for everyone in the house."

"Same applies to you; you can't play all by yourself and refuse to let another child play with you," protested Double.

Pointing towards the Wii, she then asked, "How many times has Susanna asked to play with that thing? And you never let her play, not once."

I said nothing.

"You start sharing, and we will share our food and other things with you as well; simple as that."

After saying that, Double turned away and left me standing there.

"If you listen and do as you're told, thus doing the work you have been tasked, you will not starve," murmured Double as she went into our bedroom to make herself comfortable in her corner.

I just stood there, lost for words, watching her disappear. Mum had never cooked a meal and eat it all up and leave nothing for any for us—no matter the situation. I was now convinced that Double was heartless, just because of that stunt she had pulled. After preparing myself a sandwich, I took it back to our bedroom and ate it as I confronted Double about her selfishness.

"Hey, you! Why would you cook, eat, and not leave some food for me? Mum never does that," I said in a harsh tone.

"I am not your mother. If you don't mind, I would remind you that it's way past your bedtime now."

"Well said! You're not my mother, so don't tell me what to do."

I was fuming with rage.

"You can go! No one invited you here!" I further declared, demanding, "Who asked you to cook, anyway?"

"No one. Susanna was almost dying of hunger, whilst you either didn't care or took no notice of her. So, yes, I cooked for her, not for you. Besides, for once in your life, you should have thought about other people. Your own mother is very ill, and she doesn't need any extra headache from you! Wake up! You're not growing younger. You never clean up properly after yourself. Do you have any idea what happens when you don't practice good hygiene, you allow bacteria and germs to breed, and guess what they are capable off, my friend? They can make you very sick."

"Don't call me 'my friend'. You're a toy; what do you know about friendship?" I asked.

Double had been living with us for a few weeks now. During that time, she had observed everything that happened. Evidently, she was surprised by the way I had been carrying on.

"I know enough to educate you a little bit," retorted Double.

Still not giving in, I replied, "I have no need of your education; I am fine as I am, thank you."

"If you were fine, at your age, you wouldn't need so many cavities to be filled because your teeth are going bad. So, you're not fine. I shall give you a small piece of advice, whether you like it or not."

Whilst she continued speaking, I knelt down, looked for my remote-control car, and started driving it around. I was getting tired of listening to Double going on and on. Hadn't we already had enough of that from Mum? I just didn't want to listen to any lectures about the same things, especially from Double. I wanted her out of my way, but would she move? No. I wondered what had happened to the bedtime she had been warning us about.

"All you do is play, from sunrise to sunset. You never care enough to tidy up after yourself—at least not unless someone tells you to. And not just once but a hundred times."

That exaggeration made me giggle. As I prepared myself to brush my teeth and put on my pyjamas, the car had slowed to a halt whilst I was still playing. The batteries in the remote control hadn't been charged, I realised.

Making myself cosy in my bed, I posed some questions to Double, for argument's sake: "What part of the world are you from? Don't you get it? A child's job is to play. Children can't be expected to grow up before their time; they only get one chance to be children, and that time should be used wisely. Why am I even explaining that to you? What would you know, being a toy? Besides, your purpose is for us to play with you."

"Really? I may be a toy, but I won't have false teeth in forty years' time. And you don't have to, dear friend; all you need to do is take good care of yourself by brushing your teeth properly. You won't have to get sick if you maintain good standards of hygiene. The way you live now will determine how you'll live and conduct yourself as you grow older. Practice makes perfect,"

as Double said this, she came closer to my bed and whispered into my ear,

"Being young shouldn't be an excuse for laziness and poor hygiene. Haven't you heard the saying—"

"'Cleanliness is next to godliness'," I said, interrupting her.

She went back to her corner.

"If I were you, I would strike a balance in everything I did, as I dislike being told the same thing over and over again, each and every day. Don't you suppose life would be a little bit more enjoyable if you did things differently? Try it for yourself, and prove me wrong."

Somehow, I knew she was done yapping.

"Thank you, Doctor Double, I'll bear that in mind from now on," I muttered softly through my teeth, at the same time yawning heavily.

Some of the things that Double had said made sense, although I wasn't prepared to admit it. Mum always asked us to keep clean but never explained why it was important.

"I heard that," Double retorted. "Stop being sarcastic. That attitude will never help you to be a better person and citizen of tomorrow; mark my words."

I was neither happy nor ready to change the way I did things, and I wasn't going to start taking lessons from Double. She was a toy and needed to know her place. There would be war between the two of us, if she liked. I decided to remain stubborn as I drifted off into sleep.

The next day, I was taken by surprise by the events that unfolded as the day went on. It had long been our routine that, as soon as we got home from school, we ate our snacks whilst waiting for the evening meal; and then, after our snacks, we got on with our daily chores. Though we always did our chores begrudgingly. Day after day, there was no escaping our chores, no matter how much I disliked doing them. Sometimes we would try begging Mum to let us play first, but she would refuse. Basically, she believed that it was best to establish a good routine for children as early as possible, before it became too difficult for them to change their ways. She likened it to being easier to fold a sheepskin whilst it was still new and tender, rather than later, after it had become hard and dried up.

More often than not, as soon as I could, I would start to think about tactics to use in order to avoid cleaning and tidying our bedroom. At first, Mum didn't seem to be worried about my many excuses. Soon, I began to think that I was the cleverest child in the whole wide world and could easily get away with anything, as long as it was convincing.

That day, the wardrobe was well organised, and all the clothes were placed separately and neatly.

"Wow, Mum is cool today! Maybe she got a new heart from her illness yesterday. No more chores for us—ye-e-e-e-es!" I exclaimed, jumping up and down and finally landing on Double.

My excitement was short-lived, as Mum soon called us to do our homework. Always one thing after the other. Homework finished, we had a few minutes to play. A much-welcome time of the day and my most favourite. We took to the garden to play with the rest of the new toys which Girlie-Girlie had received.

Later, Mum called us for dinner, and we raced each other to the dining room. As I settled myself on the chair, I noticed that there was an extra chair next to the table. I thought we were going to be joined by a visitor. Maybe Aunt Jenny was to join us; she had said on the day she'd left the presents that she was in a hurry but would definitely join us another day. When everyone was seated, Mum came in, holding Double, and sat her in the extra seat.

Susanna and I looked at each other in utter surprise.

Mum just looked at us, took her seat, and starting eating, ignoring our shocked expressions.

It was obvious Mum had uncovered our secret, but *how?* My heart was racing. How on earth did she find out? Did Susanna tell her? How could she? She had promised she would not tell anyone, and now she'd broken her promise. My thoughts raced in my head. Before long, I was seething with rage; a promise was a promise and should never be broken.

Double, on the other hand, looked at me with a broad smile on her face.

I wonder what she is up to. I was itching to ask my thought aloud but wouldn't dare to with Mum there, so I continued to eat, watching Double very closely.

"Thank you so very much for the lovely meal, Mum. I really enjoyed it. I would like to leave the table, if I may, please," said Susanna in a soft voice. She never did like sitting around after she'd finished eating.

"Of course you may, Susanna, and thank you for asking and for being respectful. You're such a darling, such a good girl." Mum gave her a pat on the shoulder.

Before Susanna could leave, Mum said, "By the way, you kids can bring Double into the living room, if you like. You have put a lot of effort in doing chores. I was so pleased with you yesterday for leaving the kitchen in a clean state."

Double looked at me with a satisfied expression.

"I told you that you should try it!" her eyes screamed at me.

It was then that I realised what was happening.

"Hey, Girlie-Girlie got a nice compliment before she left. I don't remember getting many of those myself," I remarked as soon as Susanna had left the dining room.

"Dee, why does it seem to bother you that Mum complimented Susanna for showing respect and table manners?"

Dad responded.

"Haven't we always told you that when you respect others, they will respect you in return? I hardly ever hear you say, 'please', 'thank you', or 'may I'. Day after day, you're told the same thing over and over again. Surely, it has to stop."

After Dad finished talking, there was deadly silence; you could almost hear a pin drop. Mum continued eating without further comment. I knew not to provoke them any further, so, as soon as everyone had finished their meal, I cleared the table and cleaned up. I then called my baby sister for a strategic meeting.

"Susanna, we need a plan. Double is right: we need to do better. Let's try to put Double's suggestion into practice and see how it turns out."

From that day forward, I made sure I did as I was told. I was getting a bit tired of having everyone on my case. They all meant well; I knew that. The previous night, I had vowed to wage war against Double, but I now realised there was no point for me to persist in keeping that resolution.

Something had to change, putting Double's theory into practice was a step forward. Do everything in moderation. When playing, I played with everything I had, and I purposed to put the same energy towards my school work and chores at home. Before long, I learnt to ask for help if I needed it. It is fair to say that there is no one who is 100 per cent perfect and doesn't make mistakes. We made lots of them, which had the potential of getting us into deep trouble with mum, but the effort we put to do things better worked in our favor.

As the weeks went by, I slowly turned into a well-disciplined child. Mum and Dad could not understand the transformation, especially when I would try to do more than I had been asked to do.

One day, Double was passing the reading table in our room, and I teasingly gave her a slight push, causing her to knock over a cup of hot milk, which Girlie-Girlie had put there to cool down (she had a habit of drinking warm milk before bed). The cup fell off the table and landed on Girlie-Girlie's foot, bouncing to the carpet—the contents splashed everywhere. As soon as it happened, Girlie-Girlie screamed as loud as she could from the burning sensation, and I jumped to my feet, running to her to check how badly she was hurt.

On hearing the screaming, Mum came rushing into our room to investigate what might have happened. As she got there, I was busy scrubbing the milk off the carpet. Once she realised why Susanna was crying, she grabbed her and took her to the kitchen in search of an ice pack to soothe the scald, which turned out to not be as bad as we thought, since the milk had cooled down a bit before it spilled.

When Mum came back, I had not only cleaned where the milk had spilled but the entire carpet. Mum stopped and looked at me.

As soon as I saw her, I jumped to my feet in a panic, attempting an apology.

"I am really sorry for pushing Double and knocking the cup off the table," I said.

"Dee, how many times do I say, 'Play nicely with others'? Now, thanks to you, another cup is ruined. Every day, something in this house gets broken; we're down to the last two cups. Do you even realise that you could have badly injured ………….?"

Mum had not finished all that she wanted to say when I interjected, "I am truly, truly sorry. Next time, I'll be more careful; I promise."

I had shown a remorseful side which I never thought I had! I loved my baby sister and wouldn't want to see her hurt.

Showing my remorseful side to the point of tearing up, took Mum by surprise; she hadn't expected that at all. Instead of getting upset, she consoled me and said that when we make mistakes, it didn't mean that we were bad people, but it did mean that we needed to remember to learn from our mistakes so that we did not repeat them in the future. I thought this was fair and wise advice.

I turned to Girlie-Girlie and apologised. Mum gave me a hug, reassuring me that it was OK. She stressed that I needed to be more mindful of others and be extra careful when doing thing.

At that moment, I realised how easy it was to apologise. This opened my eyes to a new level of understanding. I realised that apologising was, in fact, a good thing which avoided endless and unwanted arguments, and even hurting other people's feelings by saying things which are not right. By admitting my faults, I learnt that adults were more understanding and forgiving than I had thought.

We had learnt a lot from Double behind our bedroom door; she was wise when dealing with us children. Our aim was to make sure that everything which Double did or taught us became something we would do a hundred times better. After all, she was but a toy, and we had more abilities at our disposal. We figured that there was nothing that she could do that we couldn't do, if we wanted to and put enough effort into it. Susanna had always agreed and went along with anything I told her. She probably trusted me because I had long served as her mouthpiece, knowing exactly what she needed to say without her saying it. The situation with Double was no different than any in the past.

Treating Double, the way we wanted to be treated was one sign of our appreciation for having her around and learning from her. We played fairly with her, asking her permission to ride on her back, rather than just jumping on her. We gave her the same respect she gave us, and we treated her as an equal, not a toy to throw around.

It is a long-standing fact that, if you want to be loved, you have to show love and kindness to others. And if you want other people to respect you, you respect them, regardless of your age. Charity always begins at home and then spills over to other places, like school.

One Sunday afternoon, we were having a barbecue at home. Dad was overseeing the barbecue. When I went to get my food, he gave me a chicken part I didn't like.

"Dad, may I kindly change this for a sausage, please?" I asked.

He gave me the choice I had asked for, without thinking twice; at the same time, he seemed clearly surprised.

"Thank you," I said with appreciation and a smile on my face.

Later, I could see Mum and Dad whispering to each other, but I could only guess by the movement of their lips what they were saying.

"Finally! I never thought I would see the day when Dee would say, 'please', 'may I', or 'thank you'. This is a real cause for celebration!" Mum said.

"I wonder what's changed. He is no longer the same as he was. I know how hard you have tried to teach him, but it had seemed like he wasn't taking any of it into his head. The scariest thing was that Susanna always followed in his footsteps, doing exactly as he did. Though sometimes she proved to be more sensible than Dee when we corrected her. Dee's major issue was that he never cared about anything except playing. Which is good—"

"But too much playing isn't good either," Mum interjected.

"It is refreshing to see how he's now able to balance his activities."

The change was evident to them, but the cause remained a riddle.

Day after day, I did everything I needed to do without anyone telling me to do it. As soon as I woke up, I made sure my bed was made up. I brushed my teeth after every meal (I wanted health teeth when I got older). My homework was now getting done and handed in on time.

The atmosphere had changed for the better. We regularly got more compliments, along with hugs and kisses on the cheeks for good behaviour, respect, and being generally helpful.

Since changing our ways, every so often, mum would be heard using her favorite compliment, which was a rarity in the past

Daily, we heard her say, "Thank you, Pumpkins!"

With the change of atmosphere, Susanna's confidence grew. She became bolder in her self-expression and decision-making. A lot of it was a result of being told how great and wonderful she was, which she really loved, and it showed in her smiling face. At nursery school, she got involved in activities and played very well and kindly with the other children. It goes to show that, When shown love and appreciation, children become happier, and their confidence is massively boosted

Rarely would those who express charity or love fail to take it beyond their immediate family members. Usually they would express the same, above and beyond to other places and people they spend time with. That was exactly what I was determined to do. My first targeted place was my school, which I perceived to be a perfect platform. I needed to demonstrate how changed I had become. Somehow, I had a bad reputation with the teachers; in that I failed to keep quiet during lessons. I loved talking and playing and would involuntarily find myself chatting or screaming out answers, which my teachers found to be a disturbance to other students. Mum and Dad had often been called to school by my class teacher to discuss my behaviour. It wasn't that I was dull; I just lacked patience and would scream answers even before the teacher finished writing the question.

"Hey, what is the matter? Why are you looking so sad?" I asked Ben, a boy who was new in my class.

I hadn't spoken to him since he'd joined our class the previous week. I had spotted him sitting alone by the corner, seemingly unhappy, so I went over to see what the problem was.

He didn't seem to want any company, but I handed him my chocolate muffin, which he hesitantly took after I assured him that he had nothing to be scared of because we had all felt a little bit terrified when we first started. As I talked to him, he explained that he didn't think any of us wanted to play with him. He missed all his friends, and he didn't like it as much here as he did his previous school.

"Don't be sad; it's not as bad here as you might think. Everyone here is kind. Come and play football with me and my friends. That way, you'll get to know people. It'll be better than sitting here by yourself."

It took a few minutes to persuade him that we really needed another player, as we were down by one person.

"Hey, guys, meet Ben, my new friend and classmate. He would love to play."

Everyone soon warmed up to Ben, and he joined our team, creating very good goal opportunities which saw us win the game 6–1.

"Pretty awesome, huh? You should come join the school team."

The boys buzzed all over him, talking over each other, which made him feel accepted and welcome.

As I walked back to class with Ben, I reassured him that he was a good footballer and should consider the boys' invitation. The sadness was replaced by happiness as he admitted that it had been more fun playing football than sitting by himself.

"If you ever need any help with anything, don't be scared to ask; I would be happy to help you anytime."

From that day onwards, I made sure that I played and talked with those who didn't seem to be popular and probably felt that they didn't belong.

"Dean, thank you for putting the PE equipment away; that was thoughtful of you," my teacher said one day.

Instead of being the first one out the door after our PE lesson, which always came just before lunch break, I had decided to stay behind that day and help put away all the equipment we had used, rearranging the room to the way it was before the lesson. My teacher was really pleased but also surprised by my sudden thoughtfulness. I was enjoying helping out. The more I did, the more positive comments I got, which gave me more confidence and purpose. This made me less disruptive, and I even stopped screaming out answers. My teachers supported me by asking me to help other students with their homework if they were struggling a bit, as I always finished my work before everyone else.

I felt good about myself. Before I knew it, exhibiting good behaviour became second nature to me.

We were invited to a wedding that would take place during upcoming summer holidays. I was to be the pageboy, as Mum's cousin had decided to give me the honors, which would be a new experience for me. From the family photos, I knew I had attended a wedding only once, when I was a baby, and I was really excited about the prospects of being a pageboy. I had no idea what I was meant to do, but, hey, it didn't matter. As long as I didn't lose the rings or play with them, I would be all right—or so I was warned.

The weekend after school closed for the summer, Mum took us shopping for the wedding. We had to go on the bus rather than driving, which I loved. It also meant that we were going to be gone for almost the whole day, as Mum's idea of shopping was going through each and every aisle, examining (so we teased) everything on the shelves. We knew we were in for a very long and tiring day ahead of us, so the logical thing to do was to wear our most comfortable shoes. As we were leaving the house, Girlie-Girlie ran back into the house just as Mum was about to lock the door.

"Where are you going, Pumpkin? We need to go; otherwise, we'll miss the bus."

Susanna just ran straight to our room, as though she hadn't heard Mum talking to her. When she came back, pulling Double behind her, Mum gasped, asking where she thought she was taking the tiger. Mum must have known that Girlie-Girlie would take Double with her, as she did wherever she went (except when going to nursery).

"She's bringing Double with her to town, Mum; she takes her to the playground."

Habits always die hard. I just usually found myself answering for Girlie-Girlie. Time was not going to stand still for us to get to the bus stop in time, and I just wanted to go. We hardly ever used public transport, like buses, as Mum and Dad preferred drive most of the time.

"Double is coming too. We can't leave her here all alone."

The thought of parting with Double didn't seem to go well with my baby sister. Double had become her most favourite friend and companion; she was getting upset.

"Listen, Pumpkin, we will be gone for a long while, and it will be hard for you to carry Double through the day. Remember, we are not going by car but by bus, and Double is rather big to carry around town, don't you think?"

Though she didn't like the idea of leaving Double at home, being reminded of riding on the bus cheered Susanna. Double was locked in the house, with Mum assuring Girlie-Girlie that Dad would be soon back from university. The last three years had been the busiest years of Dad's life. Working a full-time job and studying for a degree at the same time, he was hardly ever at home. We were used to his absence.

Running to the bus, we managed to catch it before if took off. Once inside, we occupied the last of the seats towards the back, with too much energy up our sleeves. We could not sit still or quietly. Instead, we started singing and stamping our feet as we sang, and doing all sorts of noises and actions in the song:

> The wheels on the bus go
> Round and round, round and round, round and round
> The hooter on the bus go
> peep- peep-peep. peep-peep-peep, peep-peep-peep
> The door on the bus go,
> Come in please, come in please, Come in please
> The chairs on the bus go
> Sit on me, sit on me, Sit on me,
> the children in the bus go
> cry-cry-cry. Cry-cry-cry. Cry-cry-cry.
> Mothers in the bus go
> Yappy, Yappy, yappy
> Daddies on the bus ...

"I know what they do!" screamed Girlie-Girlie at the same time that I carried on singing, attracting the attention of other passengers.

"They sleep, they sleep. Don't they, Mum?"

"Really? I didn't know that's what they do. You tell me!" Mum said, trying to calm Susanna from her sudden, unexplained excitement, which even shocked me.

"Yes, Mum. Dad always sleeps in the car when you're driving. Doesn't he, Dee? I have seen him."

Everyone in the bus who heard her could not help but laugh.

Mum just looked at her, shaking her head and smiling.

We continued singing:

> Daddies on the bus go
> Sleep-sleep-sleep, Sleep-sleep-sleep, Sleep-sleep-sleep
> The tiger on the bus go ...

We did not finish the song, as the bus stopped at the next bus stop. As usual, some people got off, and others came in. The last person to slowly shuffle into the bus was an elderly lady who looked quite fragile. There was no seat for her to occupy, as the bus was full, and some people were already standing. She also had to stand in the passageway, just a few seats away from us.

On seeing the old lady, I thought about Double, wondering what she would have done in that instance. It didn't take me a minute to do exactly what I thought Double would have done. I had seen her in action at playparks. She was always swift to save any child in danger of getting hurt. Double did everything without being noticed, and she never sought any recognition for her kind actions. She was a wonder to behold, and I admired her behaviour.

Taking no more time to ponder, I stood up, at the same time trying to get closer to the elderly lady.

Assuming that I was getting off at the next stop, a young man prepared to take my seat.

As he was about to sit down, I turned and said, "Sorry, sir, but I was about to offer my seat to that lady over there." I pointed to the elderly lady.

The man looked embarrassed, as a good number of passengers nodded their heads as a sign of approval for my behaviour. One even patted my back.

"Rarely would anyone stand up and offer their seat to anyone these days; that's considered ancient," claimed a passenger who was standing nearby.

The elderly lady was quite grateful and couldn't stop thanking me for showing her kindness.

As the bus reached its final destination, the elderly lady stood up and walked slowly towards the exit. As she reached the baggage area, she grabbed her bags and got off, along with everyone else.

Outside, as we walked along, I noticed that a few metres in front of us was the same elderly lady, dragging her bags with great effort and looking so very tired.

I quickly thought, *Shall she continue to struggle with that luggage in this way? Surely, something ought to be done. Double would do anything in her ability and power to help her, and that's what I am going to do.*

If Usain Bolt is the fastest runner in the world, I was sure that, at that moment, I would have beaten him to the lady.

"Excuse me, but can we help you carry your bags? We don't mind helping," I said with a smile on my face, looking at the lady and pointing to Susanna and Mum.

The lady hesitated a bit, not wanting to be a bother.

But I waited for her patiently, understanding that it might be hard to trust strangers. My parents always stressed that it was not safe to talk to strangers. "Never, ever accept a ride in a stranger's car, food offered by a stranger, or an invitation to a stranger's home or a place you don't know," Dad would repeatedly tell us, but he also often said, "Surely, at time there are exempt cases where a fellow citizen might be in danger and in desperate need of help, in such cases one needs to use good judgement."

Remembering the warning about strangers, I turned towards Mum to ask for her permission.

"Mum, would it be OK to help the lady carry her bags? She seems to be going in the same direction we are."

Mum nodded her head in agreement.

"Well, I guess I can do with some help," the lady said. "Good for you for checking first with your Mum. This world is now full of dangerous people. And some can't be trusted. You seem to be a clever boy who can judge people well. But be careful always."

The lady was now echoing Dad's words; one would think they were born of the same mother.

"These bags shouldn't be that heavy to carry, but I have now celebrated more Christmases than I can count. The body has slowly succumbed to nature and ageing."

She kept talking, without stopping to take a breath, going from one topic to the next.

"My daughter in London is very ill, and I am going over to help with the little one. Her eldest daughter at eleven years old can't even boil water."

At that moment, I could not help but think about the many times when I had loathed Mum for encouraging me to learn basic cooking skills. I wondered how someone could fail to boil water. It wasn't rocket science; I was certain that even Girlie-Girlie, at the age of three, could boil water. Baffled by the way this grandmother was discrediting her granddaughter, I was ready to open my mouth to ask why she hadn't taught her granddaughter how to boil water.

Suddenly, the lady turned to me and said, "From what I have seen of you, you are one of your own kind. It is a joy to see a child who cares to think about other people, not just himself."

Her hand was now stretched towards me as she finished talking.

I didn't need to be told to hand over the bags; I got the hint straight away. We had arrived at the train station where she was to board the London train.

I handed her the bags, which she took, smiling wearily, and expressed her gratitude for my having helped her.

Mum, who had been walking very close behind us, wished her a safe journey, after which she turned and gave me one of her signature squeezy and rocking hugs telling me how proud I had made her. I could not help myself but smile as I squeezed back the hug, she had no need to emphasis need to be aware of dangerous strangers. The message had been embedded in my heart

We made sure that as the lady passed the gate barriers, she got help from the train staff onto the train, and off she went.

We then proceeded to the shops.

When we finished, Mum exclaimed,

"How pleasant! We only took a few hours to complete the shopping. I broke my own record."

We all laughed at her sarcastic remark as we sat down at Nando's for a meal which was a welcome delight to our hungry stomachs.

Give me Nando's Sunset Burger and Chips, with chicken thighs melting with cheddar cheese, and I would love you forever. We had soft drinks whilst we waited for our food to be served. Once I got my meal, I ate it very slowly, savouring every mouthful. I had developed such love for good food. and had cut down on sweet desserts in a bid to be healthy and fit.

When we finished eating, we took bus back home, where Double was waiting for cuddles, and we could not get there fast enough. Ten minutes of sitting in the disciplinary corner after a trip from town was now a thing of the past

I just could not help but wonder about what tomorrow had in store. One thing was a definite: nothing was going to stop me from achieving the highest grades in every test that I take; even the sky is not the limit. My attitude has changed, and there was nothing that could ever stop me from achieving the great things I want to accomplish. Double had challenged me to become a better person, and I was on a mission to do just that.

The daily motto I had adopted was simple:

"I, Dean, am the best I can be in anything I set my heart on, for I can do anything far better than Double, and excel at it. Period, besides Double is just but a toy"

Printed in the United States
By Bookmasters